ARTHUR'S
PRIZE☆READER

An I Can Read Book®

ARTHUR'S PRIZE★READER

By LILLIAN HOBAN

HarperTrophy

A Division of HarperCollins*Publishers*

Excerpt on pages 8-9 from *Little Bear* by Else Holmelund Minarik,
pictures by Maurice Sendak.
Text copyright © 1957 by Else Holmelund Minarik.
Used by permission of HarperCollins Publishers.

I Can Read Book is a registered trademark of
HarperCollins Publishers.

Library of Congress Cataloging-in-Publication Data
Hoban, Lillian.
    Arthur's prize reader.

    (An I can read book)
    Summary: Although Arthur loses the Super Chimp
Club contest, his pupil, sister Violet, wins the first
grade reading competition and a prize for them both.
    [1. Brothers and sisters—Fiction. 2. Reading—
Fiction] I. Title
PZ7.H635Ay 1978   [E]   77-25637
ISBN 0-06-022379-0
ISBN 0-06-022380-4 (lib. bdg.)
ISBN 0-06-444049-4 (pbk.)

First Harper Trophy Edition, 1984.

For Brom,
who is a reader and a writer too

It was a rainy afternoon.

Violet was looking at

picture books.

Arthur was reading comics.

"I am going to win

the first-grade reading contest,"

said Violet.

"The one who reads the

most books gets to win."

"You can't read, remember?"

said Arthur.

"Yes I can," said Violet.

"I can read LITTLE BEAR."

"Show me," said Arthur.

Violet read,

"It is cold.
See the snow.

See the snow come down.
Little Bear said, 'Mother Bear,
I am cold.' "

"That is easy," said Arthur.

"Now read something hard.

Read a Super Chimp Comic."

"I can't," said Violet.

"The words are too hard."

"Then you can't read,"

said Arthur.

"If you can read easy words

you can read hard words too."

10

"Show me how," said Violet.

"Read what it says here."

Arthur read very slowly,

Hurry! hurry!
Join the Super Chimp Club.
Win a picture of

KING KONG

Now you try," said Arthur.

Violet read very slowly,

"…and dinner for two
at your fav-or-ite rest-au-rant."

"Oh boy!" said Arthur.

"Dinner for two with King Kong!"

"It doesn't say that," said Violet.

"Yes it does," said Arthur.

"You just can't read hard words."

He put on his raincoat

and his hat.

He put on his scarf

and his mittens.

"Where are you going?"

asked Violet.

"I am going to be a

Super Chimp Club Super Salesman,"

said Arthur.

"If I sell the most

Super Chimp Comics

I get to win."

"Where does it say that?"

asked Violet.

"Right here," said Arthur.

15

Violet read slowly,

"Sell Super Chimp Comics
door to door!
Sign up the most kids
and win!

I read hard words," said Violet,

"and they were easy!"

"Those were not hard words,"
said Arthur, "and anyway,
I helped you."
"If I help you
can I get to be the other one
of the two for dinner?"
asked Violet.

"All right," said Arthur.

"You go get a pencil,

some paper,

and a purse

to keep the money in.

I will get a pile

of old Super Chimp Comics

so people can see

what they will get."

"I need my raincoat

and my hat too," said Violet.

And she ran to get her things.

"Whose house shall we go to first?"
asked Violet when she came back.

"My Super Chimp Comic says we have to try every house," said Arthur.

"Where does it say that?" asked Violet.

"Right here," said Arthur.

20

Violet read slowly,

"A Super Chimp salesman
knocks at every door.

Those were hard words,"

said Violet.

"No they weren't," said Arthur.

"Now let's go."

Arthur and Violet started

down the road.

"Arthur," called Norman.

"*Go-Go Gorilla* is playing

at the movies.

You want to go?"

"I can't," said Arthur.

"I am trying to win

the Super Chimp contest."

"What do you win?"

asked Norman.

23

"Dinner for two with King Kong,"

said Arthur.

"King Kong is a fake,"

said Norman.

"You can't have dinner with him."

"Wilma's big sister is in love with King Kong," said Violet. "He must be real."

"No he isn't,"
said Norman.

"Well," said Arthur,

"my Super Chimp Comic does not lie.

It says I can win dinner for two

with King Kong."

"Where does it say that?"

asked Norman.

"Right here," said Arthur.

He took out his pile of

Super Chimp Comics.

Arthur looked at the comic

on top of the pile.

But it did not say anything

about the contest.

"Help me look,"

said Arthur to Violet.

"You look at this pile."

"I can read hard words,"

said Violet to Norman.

"See, it says here,

Send for Magic Monster Kit!
Build a better monster."

"Those are not hard words,"

said Arthur.

"Where does it say about

King Kong?" asked Norman.

"I think I left that one
at home," said Arthur.

"I bet it doesn't say
dinner with King Kong,"
said Norman.
"Anyway, *Go-Go Gorilla*
is better."
And Norman rode off to the movies.

Arthur and Violet walked
down the road some more.
After a while they came
to a house.

"I will knock on the door,"

said Arthur.

"You get the pencil and paper ready."

"Wilma's big sister

baby-sits in this house,"

said Violet.

"I think she is baby-sitting now."

Wilma's big sister

came to the door.

She was carrying a baby.

"You woke up the baby,"

said Wilma's big sister.

"And you are getting mud and

rain all over the front porch.

Now go play somewhere else."

34

"We are not playing," said Violet.

"We are here to sell
Super Chimp Comics."

"If we sign up the most kids
we get to win dinner for two
with King Kong," said Arthur.

"King Kong is nothing but

a pile of old fur,"

said Wilma's big sister.

"I thought you loved

King Kong," said Violet.

"That was last year,"

said Wilma's big sister.

"This year I have a hobby.

My hobby is dancing.

See, I can dance on my toes."

She turned round and round

on her toes.

The baby screamed very loud.

"My hobby is myself," said Violet.
"I can read hard words by myself
and they are easy."

The baby screamed louder.
Wilma's big sister turned
faster and faster.
The baby screamed so loud
his face turned purple.

"Wilma can read hard words,"
yelled Wilma's big sister.
"But she does not always
know what they mean."
"I do," shouted Violet.
"They mean what they say."

"Do you want to buy

Super Chimp Comics or not?"

yelled Arthur.

"Not," shouted Wilma's big sister.

She turned round and round

very fast and slammed the door.

Arthur and Violet walked

down the road some more.

After a while they came

to another house.

There was a sign on the gate

in front of the house.

Violet said, "Arthur,

I am reading *very* hard words

on that sign and they say,

No trespassing!
Beware of dog."

"It doesn't mean anything,"

said Arthur.

"And those aren't

very hard words."

"Yes they are

very hard words,"

said Violet.

"And I know

what that sign means.

It means a very nasty dog

lives in that house

and we better not go there."

"My Super Chimp Comic says nothing ever stops a Super Salesman from making a sale," said Arthur.

44

"What does the Super Chimp Comic
say about very big nasty dogs?"
asked Violet.

"Because here is one right now!"
A large black dog came running.
He barked and growled.
He showed his teeth.

Arthur said, "Maybe we

should try another house."

Arthur started to run.

Violet ran after him.

The big black dog ran

after both of them.

"Arthur," called Violet.

"That dog can read!

He stopped at the sign!"

Arthur turned to look.

He ran right into a tree

and fell in the mud.

His pile of Super Chimp Comics

fell in the mud too.

"Now look what you made me do,"
said Arthur.

"Well," said Violet,

"whose house should we

go to now?"

"Our house," said Arthur.

"I am all covered with mud.

The Super Chimp Comics are

all covered with mud.

And anyway, that dog can't read.

He just knows to stop

at his gate.

He can't read

and you can't either!"

"Oh yes I can," said Violet.

"I can read easy words.

I can read hard words.

And I know what they mean!"

Violet picked up a Super Chimp Comic

and brushed off the mud.

"Here is one that tells

about the contest," she said.

"See, it says right here,

Win a picture of King Kong
and dinner for two
at your favorite restaurant.

That does not say you win

dinner for two with King Kong!

That says you win dinner for two.

And you win a picture of King Kong."

Violet started to walk

down the road.

"Where are you going?"

called Arthur.

55

"I am going home to read so I can win the first-grade reading contest," said Violet.

"The one who reads the most books gets to win ice-cream sodas for two at his favorite ice-cream store!"

"Don't forget I helped you
learn to read," called Arthur.
"So I get to be the other one
of the ice-cream sodas for two!"

The next day, when Violet came
home from school she said,
"My teacher says I am her best
first-grade reader.
I read the most books and
I know what all the words mean."

"That is because I helped you,"
said Arthur.
"Now let's go get the
ice-cream sodas."

Arthur and Violet went
to their favorite ice-cream store.
"What flavors do you have?"
asked Arthur.

"We have lots of flavors,"

said the waiter,

and he gave them a menu.

"Look Arthur," said Violet.

"It says here on the menu

Try our fabulous frozen
Fantasia Deluxe."

"What does that mean?"

asked Arthur.

"Oh it just means ice-cream sodas

dripping with chocolate

and whipped cream

and served over two scoops

of yummy ice cream."

"Where does it say that?"

asked Arthur.

"Right here," said Violet.

"Well," said Arthur,

"I guess I really did show

you how to read hard words."